T0198967

THE MAGICAL MYSTERY TOUR of LIFE

Written by
Tiana Barron

Balboa Press books may be ordered through booksellers or by contacting:

Balboa Press
A Division of Hay House
1663 Liberty Drive
Bloomington, IN 47403
www.balboapress.com
844-682-1282

ISBN: 978-1-9822-7833-5 (sc)
ISBN: 979-8-7652-4360-2 (hc)
ISBN: 978-1-9822-7834-2 (e)

Library of Congress Control Number: 2023912408

Print information available on the last page.

Balboa Press rev. date: 10/17/2023

BALBOA.PRESS

To my three children, Peter, Travis, and Taylor-Morgan, who, whether they know it or not, chose me to be their mother so they could learn the lessons in life they needed to experience. I love you guys more than you will ever know! The most important lesson I hope I taught you is to never be a victim, because everything happens for a reason. So just roll with the punches and grow with the knowledge.

And to my beagle, Shorty, who passed away in 2016, and my little beagle, Jaxx, because no being has ever made me feel as unconditionally loved as they have. Dogs are one of God's greatest gifts. The joy and love they give us is priceless.

Contents

Acknowledgments...vii

Listen to Your Loneliness..1

A Cry to the Heavens..3

The Land of Knowledge...7

The Book of Clowns..9

The Land of Happiness..15

Loneliness...19

Anger...25

Forgiveness...29

Rest...31

The Land of Children..37

Silence...41

Reflections..45

The Land of Love..49

The Magical Mystery Tour of Life..53

ACKNOWLEDGMENTS

I would like to thank God for creating my Universe. I realize now why he gave me such a difficult journey and why he put me on this earth: to help others, because without all the pain, I could not be so sensitive to understand others.

He gave me a beautiful gift filled with knowledge to share with the world!

I finally found the right road back to heaven.

I also would like to thank Sadiksha, who runs the Mandalas Life website (https://mandalas.life/author/sadiksha/) and is an art dealer in Kathmandu, Nepal, for the beautiful Thangka painting *Way to Heaven*. Ours is a very spiritual connection, and I would like to help her vision to preserve the monastic culture of the Himalayas.

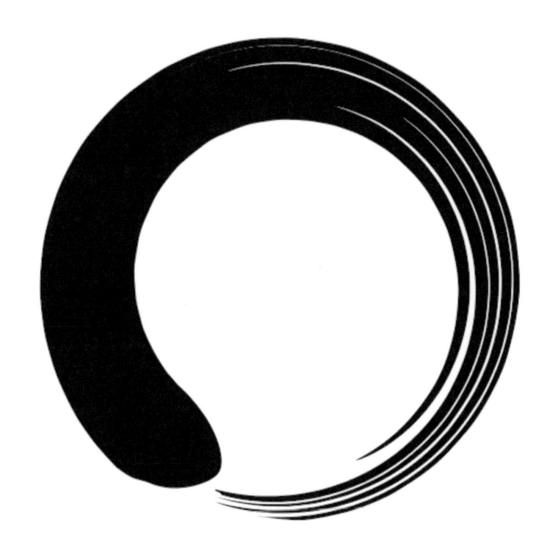

1

Listen to Your Loneliness

One day I couldn't get out of bed anymore.

I felt so sad inside. I just could not move. I lay back down and grabbed my teddy bear and began to cry. I just could not stop.

Why do I always feel so lonely inside? I feel as though there is this big empty space inside me.

I looked up to God and asked him why he didn't love me. Suddenly, I began screaming at him. I told him if he didn't love me, then why couldn't he at least allow someone else to love me? I finally cried myself to sleep.

2

A Cry to the Heavens

The next thing I knew, I was in the middle of a beautiful forest, where everything was so fertile and lovely.

Suddenly, a fox with a long fur coat appeared. He came up to me and asked, "Are you lost?"

I said, "I really do not know where I am, or even how I got here."

He looked at me and smiled. "You are in the heavenly forest."

I asked where that was. He told me it was the forest beyond dreamland.

Suddenly, in a frightened voice, I said, "I don't even know where dreamland is. I feel so lost."

"Don't feel lost. Dreamland is a place where the mind rests and your subconscious takes over. It talks to you in your sleep to help you try to work out the issues that make you sad, or happy. It's the place of your desires, fears, and dreams. The reason you're not aware of dreamland is because most people don't pay attention to their dreams. They don't realize it's their subconscious speaking to them, trying to reveal who they are."

I asked the fox how I got past dreamland. He told me God had listened to my cry for help.

"Now I must be on my way, my child."

"Wait, Mr. Fox. What do I do in the heavenly forest? I don't even know where I am."

He told me to follow the sign to the land of knowledge and find the book of clowns. And then I would begin to understand.

WHO KNOWS

OTHERS IS WISE,

HE WHO KNOWS
HIMSELF IS
ENLIGHTENED

-Lao Tzu

3

The Land of Knowledge

After meeting Mr. Fox, I began walking. Boy, was this place amazing—everything was so lush. It seemed as though I had walked for hours. I was exhausted, so I sat beside a huge tree. I looked up into a branch, and a large owl stared back at me.

He looked down at me and asked, "Are you tired?"

I smiled. "Yes, I am. I'm exhausted."

I asked him if he knew where the land of knowledge was. I presumed he would know because owls are very wise.

He looked down at me with his deep, golden eyes. He said, "If you wait until the sun sets, I will fly you there."

I was so excited. Imagine flying through the sky on an owl! I laughed because I always wanted to fly first class.

*

I dozed off beside the tree. A couple of hours went by.

The owl tapped me on my shoulder. "Wake up! It's time to go, so get on."

I got on the owl's back. The ride was the most incredible experience I had ever felt in my life. I felt peace just knowing God had heard my cries and seen my tears. It gave me the freedom to just let go.

Suddenly the owl dropped me to the ground. He told me to keep walking, that I would find my way. He told me not to be frightened because I wouldn't get lost anymore.

Those feelings were only a reflection of my soul being lost, and the peace I felt on this journey would make the reflection disappear.

4

The Book of Clowns

I walked until I reached a town. The people seemed so different from me—they were all clowns. I asked one where I could find the library.

He told me where it was and said it was only open when the moon was full.

I asked him why that was. It seemed odd that a library was only open on a full moon.

He told me only the librarian could give me that answer.

Then I asked him when the moon would be full.

"Not for eleven days."

I thanked him and kept walking, wondering what I would do for eleven days.

I walked until it got dark. I found a place to rest and fell fast asleep.

When I woke up, I found two clowns smiling at me. They asked my name and where I was going.

I explained I was waiting for the library to open. They asked what I had planned on doing until it opened. I said I really didn't know.

"Well, why don't you come and stay with us until the full moon appears¿"

"Really¿ You guys will let me stay with you¿"

"Sure."

So I went with them to their home. It was so nice to see a land of happy, giving people. They didn't even know me, yet they were willing to help.

The next eleven days taught me so much. They showed me it was easier to give than to take. I never realized that when you always take, you really lose a lot in life.

Most importantly, I had never allowed myself to really trust anyone before. And when you don't trust, you don't really experience life. I didn't want to leave their home. They were the first real family I had ever had.

*

Well, tonight was a full moon, so I would have to leave.

I looked at them with tears in my eyes. "Thank you for everything. This was the first home I had ever experienced in my life."

They seemed surprised, as though all homes were like this.

"You taught me to trust and how to give. This is a gift every parent should give their children. Thank you for giving me a home." I hugged them both and walked away.

I walked to the library with tears of happiness on my face and the feeling of joy in my heart.

When I arrived, I asked the clerk where the librarian was.

He told me to go sit down, and she would be with me shortly.

As I waited, I wondered what I would find here. A little while later the librarian came over and held up a book. She asked if this was the book I was looking for. It was the *Book of Clowns*.

I wondered how she knew which book I was searching for.

"Now read the book. And if you have any questions, I will answer them when you are finished."

Soon I began reading and quickly became absorbed in it. The story started in a land called the Land of Clowns. A village filled with people could never find happiness. They were all bitter and always complained. They lived in their sadness. It was quite a depressing place.

One day, a man heard a loud roar and followed the sound to the great sea. He saw a boat and boarded it, traveling the sea for thirty-three days. This journey was difficult as the waters were terribly rough. The man had never experienced being alone before; there was no one to complain to. He got bored and almost went crazy because he didn't know what to do with himself. He began to scream.

Finally, he noticed a book on a shelf and began reading. The book was about a girl who lived a life filled with tragedy, one devastating event after another. She was abused by her parents. She ran away from home. She was raped when she was sixteen. And she almost died from a brain tumor. Her life was filled with nothing but hardship, yet this girl always had a smile on her face, and she thanked God for each day.

The man realized what sadness truly was and then examined his own life. He felt ashamed because he really had never experienced tragedy, yet he was bitter. After reading the book, he noticed the ocean around him and saw how glorious it was. All of a sudden he saw the world differently. He thought, *Everyone has some degree of sadness, but you don't have to live in it.* It's as though he had been blind and never saw the true gifts life holds, like the ocean, the earth, and the trees, just a few of its miracles.

The man cried because he had been living as if he were the only one who existed. He was caught up in a world of his own, and he never looked around and saw the true beauty in life. Through this awareness he made a vow to try to see the wonders around him, and he laughed with abandon, like a child.

The journey was over, so he headed back to the village. On his way, an angel appeared. The angel told the man he could have one wish as a gift from the heavens for his realization on life.

He told the angel he was ashamed at how he had handled his life.

The angel looked at him and said, "First, forgive yourself. Then remember life is how you see it. If you only notice the sad things, that's how your world will appear. But you need to accept what life gives you, whatever it might be, good or bad. When you experience the bad, don't live it, just be aware of it. Life is filled with both happiness and sadness. Just don't make the sadness more important."

The angel told the man to take his wish back to the village.

When the man arrived at the village, he changed all the people to clowns because he had always remembered a clown was a person filled with laughter, even if beneath his clothing his heart was filled with sadness. A clown never showed his sadness, only tried to make other people smile and fill their lives with laughter.

After reading this book, I felt as though I was that man. I had hurt so bad inside that I never gave myself a chance to truly experience happiness. As a matter of fact, I didn't even know what happiness was.

When the librarian came by, I asked her if she had a book of happiness. She smiled and told me I would have to go to the Land of Happiness for that answer.

5

The Land of Happiness

I headed out for the Land of Happiness. When I began, it seemed like I walked for weeks; I couldn't find my way.

One day a majestic white horse approached me. She licked me, and I smiled. She seemed to know I was lost. I asked if she knew where the Land of Happiness was.

She explained that I would not be able find the Land of Happiness until I crossed the Bridge of Judgment. She invited me to stay at her ranch because she said I would need a lot of rest before I had the strength to cross the bridge. This was apparently quite a difficult task.

The horse's invitation sounded great because I was exhausted. Then she carried me across the mountain to her ranch. By the time I got there I was so tired I slept for five days.

When I woke up, I offered to lend a hand around the ranch for her kindness and for allowing me to rest there. Boy, working on a ranch was hard work! The owner of the ranch was cruel—he worked his ranch hands hard and never gave them a break. He was so ruthless, I regretted offering my help.

Three day later I couldn't take it anymore and decided to leave. I was relieved to get away from his cruelty.

I thanked the sweet horse for her kindness and asked if she could please give me the directions to the Bridge of Judgment. She told me it was about two days away. At this point I didn't even mind the journey; I just needed to get away from that mean rancher.

Two days passed before I saw the Bridge of Judgment. I was scared because it did not look too sturdy. I thought it might collapse while I crossed it. I decided to sit and contemplate crossing it.

A little while later, a very old man appeared. He came up and talked to me. I realized he was just as frightened as I was and had decided to contemplate crossing it.

The old man told me a story about an evil man who used to torture people. He even made this poor rancher be cruel to his ranch hands in order to save their lives. Suddenly I realized the man he spoke of was the rancher I had thought was so mean. I felt bad because I had judged this man without knowing all the facts. He was only being mean to his ranch hands in order to save their lives.

I had not only judged an innocent man, I had judged a lot of other people throughout my life.

I remembered how I felt when other people judged me yet never knew what truly was going on.

It brought back a memory of when my boyfriend died. I was so heartbroken that I was cold to everyone. It was only because I felt dead inside, which made me turn to anger.

This taught me that you should never judge people because no one knows what is really going on in someone else's life. Who are we to say how other people should behave?

I now saw why crossing this bridge was so difficult: because it's really hard to stop judging—especially ourselves.

Crossing this bridge is the first step to happiness because you can't start being happy with yourself until you stop judging everyone else.

As that thought crossed my mind, a mystical butterfly appeared. It spoke to me as if it had been reading my mind. "Don't be so hard on yourself. You do the best you can with life with the knowledge you have at the time. As you gain more knowledge, your choices change, just as a caterpillar changes into a stunning butterfly."

As the exquisiteness of the butterfly enhanced my thoughts, he vanished, but his memory became part of my new beginning.

This is where I must start the here and now; this is the beginning.

Suddenly I looked up and a new bridge appeared, and this one was quite sturdy. I felt a great strength inside me. I ran across the bridge with great courage, hoping to find the Land of Happiness, something we all truly deserve.

I walked, not certain which road I would take. Yet I knew I would find the right path.

Five miles into my journey, I saw several road signs. The one that stood out the most was the Village of Birth, which was three miles away.

I ran the entire way, and by the time I got there I thought I would faint.

Now that I was here, I wondered what I would find.

I saw a restaurant across the way. I decided to get something to eat, thinking it might settle my mind. When I sat down, a waiter handed me a menu.

As I read the menu, I observed how I choose which foods to order. Do we choose what we like, or do we chose what's good for us? Hopefully we like what's good for us. It was almost as if it was a menu of life. It's all about choices.

The waiter told me a gentleman wanted to buy me a cocktail and proceeded to point him out. The man was attractive and had the most incredible eyes. I accepted his offer and asked the waiter to invite him to join me.

We had the loveliest conversation about life. He suggested I go to the retreat at the end of the village. He said I would get the knowledge I was looking for. When he spoke, his eyes were filled with a tranquility that I had never seen before. His lips were filled with wisdom.

The waiter asked me if I needed anything. After I replied, I looked over to ask the gentleman if he wanted anything, but he had vanished. Several minutes later the waiter came back and told me that the man had paid for my dinner. He then handed me a note. I asked the waiter where the man had gone to, but he did not seem to know.

I read the note: "Be happy. Go find out who you are and why you were put on this earth, and then all the mysteries of life will reveal themselves. Remember that everyone is placed on your path for a reason, whether good or bad, and they will teach you about yourself. Only then can you find happiness. If you don't know who you are, you won't know what you are looking for.

"P.S. One of these days you will know who I am.

"With love."

I left the restaurant feeling sad. I really liked this man. It was as if I had met him before.

6

Loneliness

I realized when the man left, not only was I sad, I was lonely. I decided to find a hotel to spend the night before I went to the retreat.

The hotel was lovely. It was filled with magnificent antiques and works of art. The paintings were priceless. Each room had a stunning fireplace. These were rooms fit for a queen.

I decided to take a warm bath to soothe my aching body. I felt so good after, but I still seemed restless. I decided to go down to the bar and have a cognac to help me relax.

A beautiful girl was singing at the piano. The words she sang were lovely. When she finished, I complimented her on her great performance, and we talked. I asked her how she started singing and if she wrote her own material. She told me she had got her heart broken and began writing and decided to take up singing.

I saw the grief on her face. She looked how I felt inside. She was a special woman.

I looked around the room and noticed lots of lonely people.

I went back to my room because I wanted to be alone. I realized part of me loved being alone. *Then,* I wondered, *why do I feel so lonely?*

I finally fell asleep and dreamed of my childhood. I was always alone as a child. I was shy and insecure. People scared me because I was afraid they would not like me, so I created my own little world.

I woke up from my dream trying to understand all this. I turned on the light and looked around the room, and an elf appeared on a chair. It startled me.

"Excuse me if I scared you. I was sent here to keep you company so you would not be alone."

I looked up at him and explained that I really did not know what loneliness was. The elf said loneliness was a complicated matter. You can live with someone and still be lonely. That's because a lot of people don't fill their own voids and depend on others or material things to fill the emptiness they feel inside. You choose to be alone to hide in your voids, and some people hide their voids in other people. I realized the elf was absolutely right.

I told the Elf I understood what he was telling me. Even with this knowledge, I did not know how to stop feeling so lonely.

He said to me, "Don't worry about this tonight. This is something that will resolve itself through your travels in life. Even when you achieve this growth you will still have moments of loneliness, because it's part of life. There is nothing wrong with feeling lonely; just don't live or hide in it, because what you are really doing is hiding from yourself. Now go to sleep. You will need a lot of rest for your journey. I will stay here with you until you fall asleep. Give me a big hug, because I will be gone when you wake up."

Soon I fell fast asleep.

*

Morning arrived and I looked over at the chair, hoping the elf would still be there. He was gone. I was really going to miss this room. It truly was filled with magic.

I knew it was time to go to the retreat.

When I arrived there, the guardian explained that I would have to let go of everything and everyone in my past.

I would have to be totally alone with myself to enter, and I would have to sign a written commitment.

Before I signed the document I asked why I had to let go of everything. She told me I would have to trust her without question, because trust was my first lesson. So I signed the paper.

She said my second lesson would give me my answer.

"Now go to your room. In the morning your second lesson will be taught."

*

Early in the morning there was a knock at my door, and a little boy stood there. He told me to eat breakfast in the garden.

The garden was breathtaking. As I ate, an eagle appeared, and he spoke to me. I admired this amazing garden.

He smiled at me. "So you would like to know why you have to let go of your past to enter here. First, what do you feel right now?"

I told him I felt peaceful sitting in this magnificent garden.

"Is your past in this garden?"

I shook my head and laughed.

"Is your future in this garden?"

"I really don't know that answer."

He told me to look around at what was here now. He told me our past is gone and no one knows our future.

"Your past is filled with good and bad, and too often people live in the past. If they have experienced too much bad, they hold on to it and it becomes a way of life. Then they become so fearful of the good, they can't truly experience life. You need both the good and bad to be balanced."

I wondered why you would want bad in your life.

It was as if he read my mind. "You need the bad too; at times it is very painful, but sometimes it takes the pain to grow. Before the pain came there was good, but it took the pain to learn the lesson you needed to know. Oftentimes you don't realize what you're learning because it hurts so bad, but if you look back, that hurt made you let go and move on in life. Not all lessons are painful, but some have to be, because our spiritual growth is not developed enough to go forward.

"Some people's lives have been much easier than others. They haven't experienced much pain, so they must let go of their past, because they don't remember what it's like to hurt. They become insensitive to people and life. When people realize who they are, they will learn to keep their past in a sacred place, where it belongs. Then they will look at it for what it truly is. It is what has made them who they are today.

"As a young child, most of your choices were made for you. But as you grew up, you made your own choices. Whether they were good or bad, those choices were made from what you knew at the time. It is what you choose to learn from your past that is important. Then you will let go of your mistakes and look forward to your victories, which will lead you to your destiny. It might seem complicated but it's not. I am an eagle. I live in the moment where life begins."

Suddenly, the eagle flew away.

After I finished my breakfast, I decided to go for a walk. I thought about what the eagle had said to me. Everything he had said was so true. We were all like these flowers in this garden—all so different, yet all so beautiful. Flowers bloom at different times, and so do we. Flowers grow and flowers die, yet every flower brings something to this earth, and so do we.

In the peaceful silence of the garden, I realized why letting go was so important: to let go is to actually grow.

I returned to my room and felt a lovely peace just enjoying the now.

*

The evening came suddenly and I fell fast asleep.

My sleep was restless. In order to find out who I am, I had to search through my past, especially the part I had to let go of. I cried, because even though I knew the eagle was right, it's not that easy to let go of your past. I kept crying.

Then, all of a sudden, an angel appeared. "Don't cry, my child. Remember what the eagle said to you. By letting go of your past, you don't have to bury it. You just need to step away from it. Look at it as if it were a story and you are the writer. You can create new chapters and any ending you choose. It's a beginning, not an end. Turn the painful chapters into strengths and the angry moments into passions, the hate into love, and the jealousy into compassion. Turn the disappointments into desire and all your fears into joy. Keep all the wonderful parts of your past to inspire you to create a wonderful ending. Always remember: it is not what happened in the story, but how the story ends that has true meaning. Now that you have gained more knowledge about life, your past can be an amazing new beginning."

The angel left, and I fell fast asleep.

*

The next morning as I woke up, the earth was very still. A warm, calm heat appeared, and I heard all the animals talking, yet there was a silence in the world.

It was a peaceful feeling, though I knew we were going to have an earthquake. I decided to see the guardian of the retreat to let her know that this was going to happen.

She smiled at me and said, "See, my child? You are in tune with life. Just use this knowledge to learn your next lesson. Go now and be still."

I went back to my room. I wasn't afraid. As a matter of fact, I was filled with a peaceful feeling inside. When I sat on my bed, the earth shook. The pictures on the walls fell to the ground and broke. I almost enjoyed the earth shaking. It made me feel that life shared the anger I still carried inside, which made me realize how angry I was. All the disappointments were still very much alive inside me. I was bitter that none of my dreams had become a reality. I had let go of my past, but not the anger that came with it.

24

7

Anger

The day had ended with an eclipse of the sun. It was strange how the clouds covered the sun with darkness, yet the darkness never left the earth. There was no light. I wondered what was going on in the universe.

I decided to see the guardian again. She explained that this was my next lesson. "When you learn the answer as to why the earth is dark, you will see the light again. You must find the answer yourself."

I returned to my room. I was afraid I would go outside and the earth would be covered with darkness. I just could not find the answer. Then my frustrations turned to anger. It made me realize how important this issue was. What was its real purpose?

I decided I had better relax because anger makes me crazy: my whole body aches, and my head feels like it's going to explode. It feels as if I am trying to get out of my body.

I went for a walk to alleviate some of my stress. Walking also allows me to think clearer. I must have walked for hours but the anger I felt would not dissipate. It made me feel angrier. What a terrible feeling this was. The world seemed so dark. It was almost as if I created the earth's darkness through my anger.

What I felt was what seemed to exist. Then I felt terrified of myself and all the darkness. These were feelings I had always suppressed. They seemed so foreign, yet they were hidden inside me my whole life. Finally, as I grew older, I became unhappy about the littlest of things. But it really wasn't these things that made me mad; I had been suppressing the anger.

I knew this was the dark side of my soul. If you stay there too long, you will become bitter.

Days passed, and nothing seemed to change, so I prayed to God for help. I felt like I was a prisoner of the dark side of life.

One day, a wise man appeared. He was dressed in a brown robe and wore a turban decorated with golden beads with a ruby in the center. He had a long white beard and walked with a Golden Wand. He asked me what I was searching for. I told him I just wanted to stop feeling so angry. I realized it could destroy me.

"Yes, this is true. This emotion has destroyed a lot of people. This is the reason people have killed each other, and one of the main reasons people take drugs. It is also why people have created diseases like cancer and heart attacks. This is also the reason there is child abuse, rapes, and wars. I could go on and on. This is one of the weakest sides of humanity and is the most dangerous side. You see, when you get angry, you lose all clarity. The darkness takes over."

The wise man asked me to take a journey to the Land of Childhood with him. He told me this was the beginning of our adoption to anger.

"Now close your eyes and you will travel back to your childhood. Now that you are there, what do you see?"

I thought for a moment about what I was seeing. "A little girl filled with sadness."

"Do you feel sad?"

"Yes. I feel like I have been denied love, but I don't know how to deal with my feeling, so I suppress them. I don't know how to get angry because it scares me. It represents the hate my parents shared. I decided to deny myself anger."

"This allowed a dark shadow to live and grow inside you. It covers your soul like a disease, and that disease has denied you of the one thing you have been longing for your whole life: love."

As I woke up from my childhood, the wise man whispered to me, "There is nothing wrong with feeling angry; it's part of your soul. But to deny its feeling is what is dangerous, because then you cheat yourself out of who you are. If you had allowed yourself to get angry as a child, you would have gotten angry for the right reasons as an adult. A lot of children suppressed this feeling, and that's why they grew up so angry. Then they become self-destructive adults. The destruction leads to endless disappointments because then your choices in life are made out of need and not true desire. What you need to do is heal your soul, and then you need to adopt yourself—as if you were your own parent."

"How can I do this?"

"We all have an inner child. Raise yourself the way you would like to be raised. Be your own parent."

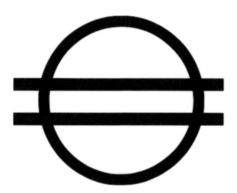

8

Forgiveness

"Before I go," the wise man said, "I want you to consider one important thing: Forgive your parents for the way they raised you, because they did the best they were capable of with what knowledge they had about life.

"One of the most important qualities of being a good parent is forgiveness, and you must forgive your parents before you are granted the right to adopt your inner child. If you can't forgive them, you will never be able to forgive yourself."

I looked around. The wise man was gone.

I closed my eyes and called out to the universe. "I forgive you, Mommy and Daddy," I repeated over and over.

When I opened my eyes, the world was light again. Now I saw the world in a different way. I knew that I had been living in bondage, because I could not let my energies flow by not being able forgive. That was why my body always seemed to ache.

What is really scary is how we deceive ourselves. I always thought I had forgiven my parents.

9

Rest

With all this on my mind, I headed back to my room. I realized I had obtained a lot of great knowledge and became overwhelmed. Learning is one of the best parts of life because you see the world so differently. All this knowledge made me want to lie down and rest.

I slept for ten days. My body just needed to lie there to be free. I tried a number of times to get out of bed but didn't have the strength. I wondered how I could be so full of knowledge yet too tired to live it.

One day there was a knock at my door; it was the guardian. She looked at me with sorrow. She told me she had noticed that I hadn't been around and decided to check up on me.

"You look worn down, my child."

I replied, "I'm weak and feel like I don't have any life left in me. I don't understand all this. I've obtained some of the greatest knowledge in life, and instead of feeling happy, I feel dead."

She explained that the old life energies were dying in me in order for the new life to exist.

I began to cry. "I have become a fictitious character to people and myself so I could deal with all the hurt I experienced. I realize now that I am just a little girl in search of love, and not the tough free spirit I appear to bc."

"Don't worry; most people create characters in order to survive their trials in life. It just makes them feel more comfortable with themselves. You see, once you know who you are and accept it, you will treat yourself with the love and understanding you deserve. That's why you have to adopt yourself—because you're the only one who knows what you need. The reason you feel so tired is that you finally gained enough spiritual knowledge to know you cannot be who you aren't. It will only harm you. You never saw it before because you were so filled with hurt and anger that it buried your heart. Now that you know the truth, it's like you are naked and the clothing you wear can't hide your true soul anymore."

"My child, this is not an easy task you have taken on. Just because you have learned some of the mysteries of life doesn't mean you know how to play the game of life. You are just learning the rules. Your soul will be much calmer with this knowledge. Total peace comes at different times for everyone. It will come when your soul is ready for heaven. Some people have to live through several lifetimes to go home. Patience, grasshopper."

She smiled at me before continuing. "The first step is to rest. Treat yourself like a newborn and pamper yourself. When you are ready to walk, you will. I'm leaving now, but if you need me, ring the bell. Don't ever be afraid to need someone, because that's your inner child crying out for help. Too often people are ashamed to show their need for others; they are afraid they might appear weak. There is nothing wrong with being weak—you are only human. We are all weak at some point. If you deny yourself weakness, you will never be able to give yourself what you need, which is important. It shows that you care about yourself. It might be hard at first, because when you gave yourself what you needed before, you were giving the character you created what she needed. But that character wasn't a healthy soul, so you gave it unhealthy things. Now that you have given life to yourself, you will give yourself loving things. Rest, my child. Just rest."

*

Days passed. I became very sick and couldn't get out of bed. I did not even have the strength to walk out to the lovely garden. I realized my body was trying to tell me something. I needed to slow down and give life a rest.

Weeks passed, and I became frightened because I was still so weak. I decided to ring for the guardian and ask her if she could send a doctor to look at me.

She arrived and gently rubbed my head. "I will send the healer to take care of you. Don't be afraid."

About twenty minutes later the healer arrived. He was a very old man, but his smile was as pure as a child's. "How are you feeling?"

"I am so tired, and I'm afraid I'm going to die."

He examined me. "You will be fine. Just stop worrying so much. This is your time to rest from life. What are you so worried about?"

I explained about all the knowledge I'd learned about life, and how this realization made me exhausted. "I have been living life a certain way, always trying to get approval from everyone. I was living for everyone else and not me. Now that I have a new life, I'm not certain who I really am or what I want to do when I grow up."

He looked at me with a grin. "Very few people know what they want to do when they grow up. Don't worry about this now; it will come to you when the time is right. Just give yourself life as if you were giving birth to yourself. A baby sleeps in its mother's womb for nine months in order to rest for the journey into life. You are still an unborn child who needs to heal and rest within yourself. The day your body is strong again, you will be reborn. Just remember, you are your true parent. Give yourself what you would give your own child."

Then he gave me a big hug and told me this was the first thing I should give myself. He was such a kind soul filled with so much wisdom.

I knew I needed a lot of rest, but this man gave me the security to give myself life. Patience was the first step I needed to take right now. I needed to let go of my frustrations and be patient with myself.

Before the healer left, he said to remember this: "No one will fail at what God appointed you to do, and when you forget, remember this: he will walk beside you. Just look at the sky and know he is always with you."

After he left, I realized this was how I got lost in the first place: I stopped having faith. For the first time, the subject of past lives made sense to me. If this was all my past, I had to find out its purpose and what I learned from it.

What stood out the most was realizing you must be true to your own soul, not someone else's. Your soul is the key to the heavens. When you live your life through others, you lose sight of your soul.

I could give my inner child a head start in life by keeping my best qualities so I will have a direction, and the lesson I have learned will help guide me to the right roads.

Now I would rest because I saw its true significance. Your body is your vehicle, and when it has traveled to such dark corners, it needs a complete overhaul. The miles devoted to stress alone would blow out the engine. I realized I hadn't put proper maintenance on my vehicle. I had taken the physical side of myself for granted. The world seemed to move so fast now. We forget what year our vehicles were made and how tough the roads have gotten.

It all starts at the beginning—and loving yourself. The body frames the soul, and we must protect it. Not only must we protect it, we should be proud of it. This was something I had never been proud of because I never felt beautiful. My mother always told me how ugly I was, and unfortunately, we base our thoughts on what society believes to be beautiful. Because I was different, I never saw my own beauty. I truly was living in the world and not with God, because whatever God makes is beautiful. We are all his beautiful creations.

When you become your own parent, you sure see yourself differently. You see yourself as God sees you. You start treating yourself with love and respect. Now I could stop judging myself and give myself the encouragement I needed, because I would want my child to have a fantastic life and live her dreams.

I still felt tired, but my mind was finally able to have a little peace. This was something I hadn't felt in years.

I looked out the window at the falling rain. I was amazed at how hard it was pouring. The storm made me feel weaker because I longed for the sun. I knew then the world was really changing; even the earth cried out for peace.

I felt like a restless infant driving myself crazy. Now I know why they call it the terrible twos. I started laughing. I wanted to call up my own mother and apologize for being hyper. That was what made me decide to start my life at a much slower pace and just enjoy the rain. Otherwise I would always be waiting for something else to happen to make me happy, instead of what is right in front of me.

Several days went by, so I tried to get out a little even though I was still weak. I got absorbed just watching the earth and every little part in life I could see. It was great to get away from myself and watch the world evolve. It's amazing how, once we get out of ourselves, the world seems so intriguing and quite funny. It's as if you are watching a movie, and when you look at life this way, the pain seems to disappear. I spent my days doing whatever made me happy. This helped me learn a lot about myself.

One day I decided to find out where the Land of Children was. So I rang the guardian, because I knew she would have the answer. She explained that I could go there in a few weeks. I needed to rest a bit longer first.

Three weeks passed, and the guardian sent the healer to look at me. I told him I was anxious to go to the Land of Children. I felt this was where everything began.

"You are a spiritually gifted girl and truly aware of life, but you must rest a bit longer before you can go."

I looked at this gentle man and told him I knew he was right. There was one thing that I learned from my travels: never rush things, because timing is crucial, and if you rush something, you may lose it.

About one month later there was a knock at my door. A little boy wearing a tuxedo and a huge top hat stood there. "Your coach has arrived, ma'am."

I looked out and saw a huge coach shaped like a pumpkin. The horses were silver. I felt like Cinderella going to the ball. I knew it was time to visit the Land of Children.

10

The Land of Children

The journey took five days.

My young driver said, "Ma'am, look ahead. We're almost there." I looked up and saw a breathtaking castle that was right out of a storybook.

The coach stopped and I asked the boy why.

"This is the Land of Children."

My eyes lit up with tears of joy. Why, of course. Who would be more fitting to live in a castle but children?

We entered the yard, and I felt like I was visiting every part of the world. Children from every country imaginable were here.

*

I got settled in and rested for a few days. Then I went out and played with the children. This was truly one of the most fun times I have ever experienced in my life.

The most incredible part of it was that, when children are raised together, they never learn prejudice. They see each other's souls, not their color or race.

As that thought crossed my mind, a teacher appeared. "Hello, my dear, and welcome to the Land of Children. Would you like to join me for some tea?"

"Yes, thank you very much."

"I have heard some lovely things about you."

I smiled. She told me I looked like I was in a daze and wondered where my mind was off to. I told her I felt like I was somewhere between childhood and adulthood.

She laughed but then looked at me very seriously. "What would you like to learn here?"

"First, I just want to play and be a child, for many different reasons. The main reason is because I never really had a childhood, and I feel childhood holds the answers to life."

The teacher told me to go play with the children for as long as I would like, and when I was ready, I should return to see her. "We would be proud to have you stay with us. This can be your home as long as you like."

*

Day after day I had a great time just playing, and not having any responsibility. I made all kinds of friends. It was quite interesting. One of the best things about children is that they are honest whether they are cruel or nice; their responses are of truth. They respond in the moment and not from excess baggage.

Yet I realized some children aren't as fortunate because they came from severely abusive homes, which didn't allow them to ever truly be children. I knew this was one of the answers I was looking for and one reason we have so many dysfunctional adults—they were never allowed to be children, and your childhood is where you get your basic makeup. Your trials and tribulations evolve you into the kind of adult you will become. This was truly one of the most valuable experiences I had learned through my travels

Time seemed to pass quickly. I realized the freedom of being a child was great, but I seemed to have become unfocused. My mind could not stay in one place too long, and my attention span was tiny.

Suddenly, I realized I needed to discipline my inner child.

This was something a lot of people have issues with. Either they had too much or too little, depending on how you viewed it. Discipline was hard for me. I am not very good at it. I guess I was afraid of it because it gave a direction that made you have to make a choice, and I never seemed to make very good choices.

I'd had so many traumas, I stopped knowing what I truly wanted from life. So I decided to discipline myself. The first thing every morning I would wake up and speak with God and ask him to walk with me so this journey wouldn't be so difficult. Also, by talking aloud to myself, I began to listen to my heart.

The subject of discipline was even harder for me than I had ever imagined because I'd been living on my own since I was fifteen—a child trying to live life as an adult. By the time I really became an adult, I had spent so much time just surviving I never went through nature's process.

This made me realize I needed to spend time alone with myself for a while. I was depending on others to fill my voids. There is nothing wrong with needing other people sometimes, but to live for others will destroy you. You'll end up bouncing off the walls after a while.

11

Silence

I went back to the teacher and told her I would leave the Land of Children tomorrow. I thanked her for her kindness. She asked me where I would travel to next. I told her I was headed to the Land of Self.

The next day I headed for the Land of Self. The teacher had a coach ready to take me.

The driver told me this ride would take eighteen days, and after that I would have to take a train to a town called Nirvana. I asked him if this was the town of Self.

"No, it's not, but it is the village from where you can take a ferry that will take you to the Island of Self."

I was so excited. I had always dreamed about going to an island.

Two weeks passed, and we arrived. I hugged the sweet coach boy and said goodbye and thanked him for all the help he had given me.

He told me to go to the dock to catch the ferry. When I arrived at the ferry, a penguin stood at the gate.

I told Mr. Penguin I wanted to go to the Island of Self. I didn't see a ferry, though, and I thought maybe I had missed it. I asked him when the next ferry would arrive.

He said, "Come with me. This is what will take you to the island."

My mouth must have dropped to the ground—he was pointing out a whale. "You mean a whale is going to take me to the island?" I exclaimed.

"Why, of course. This island is sacred, and only God's creations can enter it."

What an adventure this was. I was quite nervous, but this was sure different.

The whale spoke to me. He explained that when we reach the island, a map would lead me to the hut that would be my new home. It will be filled with enough food to last my visit. It was strange because I was afraid. Being alone is quite frightening because you have to face yourself. Your truths, your lies. Maybe we should ask ourselves the key question to life: "What is my purpose?"

I think that's where a lot of us get lost between ourselves and our purpose, because you have to get out of yourself to find your purpose. We are either too involved in ourselves or not involved enough, so we lose our purpose.

The island was the most stunning and peaceful place I had ever experienced. It was so easy just to relax, it made me realize what a truly beautiful universe God had created.

My days were filled with lying in the sun and reflecting on the peace the ocean brought me. I thought I could stay here forever. Nature filled my voids with joy.

I realized, as the world progressed with science and modern conveniences, that was where a lot of us got lost. We either tried to survive or compete.

Money, fame, and power tore the world apart. There is nothing really wrong with any of it, but most people don't know how to deal with their karmic presence. Including myself. I had a life filled with a lot of pain, and instead of accepting my road, I fought all the way.

Part of this was good because I became a survivor. The bad part was that it made me become someone I wasn't, so I always felt lost and lonely. I wasn't really me.

That's what loneliness really is, not being yourself. You have to be able to be with yourself before you can be with anyone else. This is why so many relationships don't work out, because most people haven't found peace with themselves, so how can they share love with someone else?

Today was Easter, a perfect day for a new beginning. This was the day Jesus rose from the dead. This day is a perfect symbol of giving ourselves a new life.

It's funny, but learning to be alone with myself was actually a great revelation. I always believed in God but had stopped living it.

I don't believe in religion because everyone has different methods to be close to God. The real way to be close to God is not through man's teachings but by living in God's kingdom.

The most important thing the Lord asked of us is to be ourselves. He knows we are not perfect; we are just children trying to find the road to the heavens. We must find and accept our destiny, because this is the way to show God that we have faith.

I planned to stay on the island for a while even though I found the peace I was seeking.

12

Reflections

The time had come to make my knowledge a reality, so I headed to the Land of Reflections.

I went to the water and the whale was waiting for me. It was quite strange; he knew I was ready to leave and where I was headed. There are no coincidences in life. Everything happens for a reason, and when the time is right, things are already there. We don't have to ask for them.

I wondered what this place would be like. As we approached land, the whale told me I had great courage and that this would finally lead me to my destiny because I valued life enough to seek its meaning.

"There will be a limousine to take you to the Land of Reflections. God knows that all the lessons are wearing on you. Now that you are willing to get out of yourself and accept your life, he wanted you to be driven first class to your next journey."

The ride was great. I could just relax and enjoy the scenery, even though I thought it was a bit odd.

The driver stopped and let me out, and a film director was waiting for me. He took me to a screening room and told me to watch this film—my life story. The film started on the day I was born and ended the day I decided to seek the mysteries of life.

"You should pay close attention to every moment of your life. Watch and see how every incident led you to a new path."

I watched. It was dramatic reliving the pain. I cried aloud. When the film was over, I felt good because even though I had made a lot of mistakes, I always kept trying.

It also showed me that the choices I made were the choices I had to make to just keep going. Now that I had accepted my life, I could really enjoy it more because I understood the game of life.

When the lights came on, the director said, "Now we're going into the editing room so we can watch the film again, and you can edit your life so you can make a new film on your life story. This way, even if you've had hard roads, you can create the ending you want. Now you can be the director of your life."

Now I know why reflecting is so valuable. It shows you your purpose, if you really look at it. It's like a puzzle. If you put your tragedies and victories together and piece them in the right order, you will find the answer when you complete the puzzle.

The director invited me to lunch, and we shared our experiences. He told me when he watched his own film, he made a list of priorities in life to achieve his destiny. He suggested I do the same. Then he asked me what the strongest message I had learned about my life through the film was. I told him I had a great desire to love and be loved.

He told me I should go to the Land of Love. This would be the beginning of my new life because once I fulfilled this desire, everything else would come to me.

"Before you go there, I want you to stay here and watch some other people's life stories. Everyone has different desires, and this will help you understand others better."

He was absolutely right. The more films I saw, the more it showed me that everyone had a different destiny. This is why you can't take things personally, because everyone is trying to find their own path.

Well, the time had come, and I was excited because I was going to the Land of Love. I knew this would be the most important lesson in life for me to understand.

13

The Land of Love

I thought about what I was seeking. I was uncertain where I might find the Land of Love. Love has so many meanings, yet I felt it was the biggest void in my life. I had traveled so many roads trying to find this place I call love. I actually had been so desperate to fill this void that I had placed my life in the hands of others, hoping someone would love me. Yet I always seemed to find people who couldn't even love themselves, so how could they love me?

Yes, that was the mystery. I hadn't loved myself, so I was attracting people like myself. The world I lived in was the mirror of my soul. How can you love me if I can't love myself?

I think the real problem was that I had such a strong desire to be loved. I walked around my whole life blind to its reality.

As my mind was deep in that thought, my Guardian Angel appeared. I wasn't surprised that I had one, because how could I have kept traveling this road of life if I hadn't? I would have collapsed years ago.

My Guardian Angel placed me on her wings so gently and rode me to the heavens. I always knew heaven would be like this. It's your very own fairy tale.

My Guardian Angel suggested we make some potato soup, so we began peeling potatoes.

She said, "Remember when you went to the Land of Reflections and you saw your life on the screen?"

I nodded.

"What did you see that made you seek love? What was the beginning?"

I thought for a moment before clearing my throat. "I learned about hate because that's how my parents lived their lives."

"Well, my child, how do you think you can share love if you really don't know what it is?"

"Through my travels I found the beginning of love. It's unconditional, for better or worse, and you don't have to get it back. I met a man who I loved very much, and although he was incapable of loving anyone yet, he was sweet. It didn't make me love him any less, because I didn't take it personally. Yet it was my beginning, because even though I never knew what love really was, I felt these whispers from my soul that this was part of it."

"Yes, it is. Isn't that man a reflection of your past? You learned to unconditionally love through him. This was the key to opening the mysteries to your life. Now you must unconditionally love your inner child, and your destiny will reveal itself. Part of loving yourself is trusting the life God chose for you. I know sometimes it's difficult, because some roads are really dark. But this is all part of the Land of Life, and not until we fulfill this journey may we live in the heavens."

It's funny, but I had been traveling all over the planet to find something that was within me the whole time. I now understood why you had to adopt yourself. What you are really doing is loving and accepting the soul that lives within you, and giving life to yourself.

I stopped feeling so lonely now because I had, inside me, what I thought existed in someone else.

The Land of Love gave me the wings to fly through life, and it gave me the knowledge that I needed to strengthen my interior life. Only when my soul is strong enough will I accomplish my journey.

The most important message my Guardian Angel gave me was, "What is for you will not pass you." These are the words I leave to the world.

Yes, at times we all feel cheated with life, but if we remember these words:

What is for you will not pass you

we will realize we haven't been cheated at all, because we all have a different cross to bear. If we love ourselves, we can fulfill the destiny God gave us. With this faith, we can learn to love each other and one day all share the joys of heaven.

14

The Magical Mystery Tour of Life

I am giving you the golden ticket to the magical mystery tour of life. I know this is my greatest purpose in life—to share the knowledge God has given me.

When you wake up each morning, say "Thank you" for every breath you take. These two magical words will change your life!

Now take your *golden ticket* and go ride the *merry-go-round* and take the tour of your life, and remember to always stop and be *grateful* for your *magical journey* that God gave you.

Printed in the United States
by Baker & Taylor Publisher Services